A BROKEN CRAYON STILL COLORS

DANIELLE MAZZILLI

A Broken Crayon Still Colors

iUniverse books may be ordered through booksellers or by contacting:

iUniverse
1663 Liberty Drive
Bloomington, IN 47403
www.iuniverse.com
844-349-9409

Danielle Mazzilli
20 Broad Street, 1807
New York, NY 10005
(914) 420-0536
mazzilli.danielle@gmail.com

ISBN: 978-1-6632-3503-9 (sc)
ISBN: 978-1-6632-3505-3 (hc)
ISBN: 978-1-6632-3504-6 (e)

Library of Congress Control Number: 2022900953

Print information available on the last page.

iUniverse rev. date: 01/19/2022

"For all broken crayons,
may you continue to color."

She ran up to her room and
pulled us out from her drawer.
She had tears in her eyes,
but none of us were sure.

She spilled us out, falling onto her desk. Tears still rolling down her cheek and streaming down her neck.

"Why are you sad?" I asked as a blue crayon does. The girl just stared, then sighed, "Because."

"Is it something I can help with?" asked the red crayon. "Please, give it a whirl!"

"Because why?" my fellow yellow crayon questioned the girl.

The girl looked up and said, "I'm not so sure. I just know my grownups won't be living together anymore."

"They told me they loved me,
and that their love will never
change. But now my family
portrait will look very strange."

"Oh dear", sighed the purple crayon, "We can help with that. You see, every family looks different, even a family of cats."

The girl picked me up and held me tightly in her hand. "We're here to help", I told her, "a whole box of crayons."

"There is something I want to
tell you", said the orange crayon
with glee. "A broken crayon
still colors, yes, even me!"

The girl smiled and pressed my top down on her paper. She started drawing clouds and a sky, then told me she'd be back later.

The girl kept her promise and came back after she ate. She grabbed the green crayon and shouted, "It's time to create!"

With the green crayon, she drew
some grass and a few leaves.
She picked up the brown crayon
and started drawing tall trees.

Before I knew it, her background was done. "I think I'm forgetting something", she said. "Oh yeah, the sun!"

She picked up the yellow crayon
and drew a circle in the corner.
She added some rays, then
stars around the border.

And just as her creation was
starting to come to life, she set
us down and asked for advice.

"How can I draw my family, now that
my grownups are apart? I really need
your help. I don't know where to start."

"Remember what the orange
crayon told you before? A
broken crayon still colors", I
told the girl once more.

The pink crayon exclaimed, "I have an idea! Leave some spaces, here, here, and here."

"There is another thing I think
you should know. Families are
meant to grow, grow, grow."

The girl did as the pink crayon
described. She drew her
family, and kept space in mind.

It had been a few days, maybe
months, or a year. Timing for
crayons is a little unclear.

But the girl came back with some
news to share. "The best thing
happened!", she did declare.

"I have a bonus mom and a bonus dad too! Everything you said about a family growing is really true!"

So then the girl drew in her new family members. She filled in the spaces. "Yay, you remembered!"

"I even have a stepbrother and four stepsisters, you see. And the best thing about this is I love them and they love me!"

The girl picked up the red crayon and drew some hearts around her family. "My family portrait is now complete!", she said very happily.

"Thank you so much for helping me see. That the spaces on the paper were to be filled with people who love me."

"A family comes in all sizes, shapes, and colors. And sometimes they change like seasons. Fall, to winter, then spring and summer."

The girl grabbed some tape to hang her picture on her mirror. She wanted to keep her growing family near her.

Before she packed us away, she put her hand on her heart. She sat back and smiled, admiring her art.

"If you ever feel sad, confused, or scared. Remember everything we have shared."

Then the girl placed us back in her drawer. "A broken crayon still colors. That is for sure."

MY FAMILY PORTRAIT